If You Were a Parrot

By Katherine Rawson

Illustrated by Sherry Rogers

In memory of Richard—KR

To my brother Bill, who made me laugh more than anyone I have ever known—SR

Thanks to educators and scientists at SeaWorld and the National Aviary for verifying the accuracy of the "For Creative Minds" section.

Publisher's Cataloging-In-Publication Data

Rawson, Katherine.

If you were a parrot / by Katherine Rawson ; illustrated by Sherry Rogers.

1 v. (unpaged) : col. ill. ; 23 x 27 cm.

Summary: Just what does a parrot do all day? Children imagine what life would be like as a pet parrot. Includes "For Creative Minds" section with parrot fun facts, tips for taking care of a pet parrot and a make-a-beak craft.

ISBN: 978-0-9764943-9-3 (Hardcover)

ISBN: 978-1-6071811-8-7 (pbk)

Also available as eBooks featuring auto-flip, auto-read, 3D-page-curling, and selectable English and Spanish text and audio

Interest level: 004-008

Grade level: P-3

Lexile Level: 640 Lexile Code: AD

1. Parrots--Juvenile literature. 2. Parrots. I. Rogers, Sherry. II. Title.

SF473.P3 R39 2006

636.6/86/5   2005931004

Manufactured in China, January, 2010

This product conforms to CPSIA 2008

Second Printing

Sylvan Dell Publishing

976 Houston Northcutt Blvd., Suite 3

Mt. Pleasant, SC 29464

If you were a **parrot**, you would have two feet, just like you do now, but... you would only have **four toes** on each foot, and two of them would point **backwards.**

With feet like these, you could climb everywhere . . .

up the curtains,

all around the bookshelf,

in and out of boxes,

FRAGILE
THIS SIDE UP

even **to the top** of a potted fig tree.

wooden spoons,

If you were a **parrot,** you would have a sharp, hooked beak. To keep your beak in shape, you would have to chew things . . . **pencils,**

the legs of chairs,

and maybe even the entire

telephone directory.

Your favorite food would be sunflower seeds and nuts.

You would use your hooked beak to **crack** them open,

just like that.

You would like
fruit and
vegetables, too ...
corn on the cob,
oranges,
watermelon,
and
**especially
broccoli.**

You might even enjoy an occasional popsicle—

stick and all.

But your family probably wouldn't let you eat at the table.
You would have to have your dinner **in your cage.**

If you were a **parrot,** you would make lots of **noise.**

You would **squawk** when you were happy and **screech** when you were mad.

You would **squawk** and **screech** some more just to pass the time.

You might also learn to copy people's words. You might say

"Hello!" and **"Wanna popsicle!"**

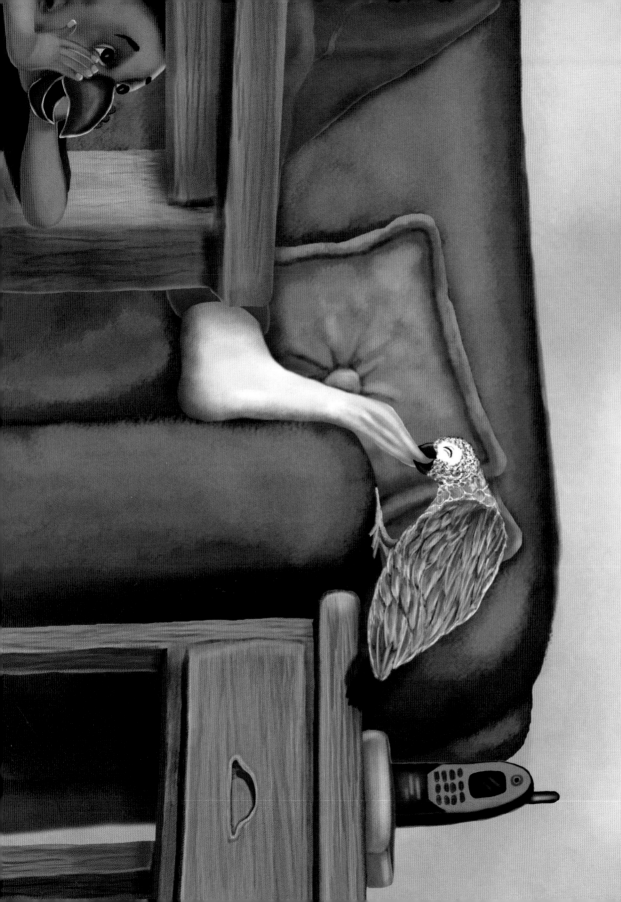

If you were a very clever parrot, you could copy other sounds too.
You might make a sound like a **telephone ringing . . .**

... everyone in your family ...

Then you would **laugh** when ...

...**ran**...

...to answer the phone.

If you were a **parrot,** you would love to bathe.

You would shower under a **spray bottle** or take a bath in a **dish.**

You would have so much fun that you would **squawk** and **splash** water **everywhere.**

Afterwards, you would **preen** all your feathers carefully, one by one.
Then you would look in your mirror and say **"pretty bird!"**

chewing,

At the end of the day after

climbing,

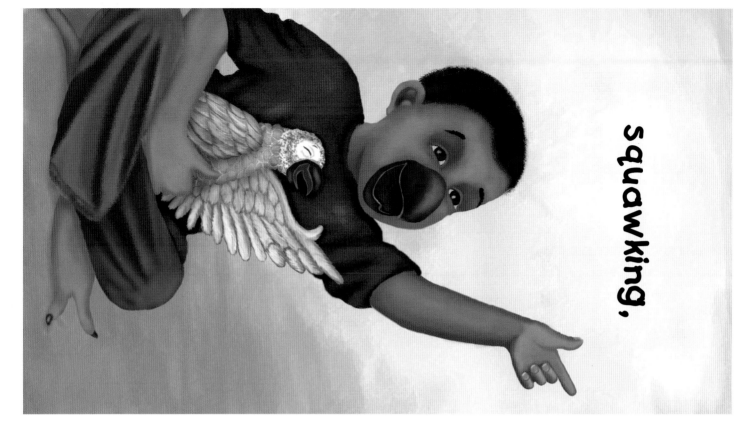

squawking,

and **preening;**
you would be very tired.

Your family would put the cover on your **cage.** You would settle down on your **perch** and **ruffle** up your feathers.

You would put your head under **your wing** and you would sleep like that all night long . . . *if you were a parrot.*

For Creative Minds

What is a Bird?

Just like you might sort candy or cereal by color or shape, plants and animals can be sorted or classified into groups. Parrots are animals in the "Aves" class, which means they are birds.

Birds come in all different shapes and sizes but all birds have feathers. In fact, they are the only animals that have feathers.

Birds are warm blooded, just like us. That means that they make their own body heat.

Birds don't have teeth; they have bills or beaks. The shape of the beaks depends on the type of food they eat.

All birds hatch from eggs.

The feathers help them to fly (although not all birds can fly) and to stay warm. Feathers are made out of keratin, just like our hair or fingernails.

Like us, birds have a backbone. Some of their bones are hollow, and lighter, to help them fly.

Parrot Adaptations

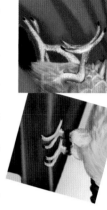

Parrots have beaks that are strong enough to break through hard seeds or nuts. *Could you open a nut (walnut, pecan, or Brazil nut) with your teeth?*

The bottom part of the top beak has little ridges to help hold the nuts or seeds while they break into them. This is similar to the ridges in a nut-cracker that we might use to open a nut.

Parrots have four toes—two toes face forward while two point backwards. This helps them to hold onto tree branches and their food. They can use their back toes like we use our thumbs.

Parrots also use their beaks to find food hiding under the bark of trees or in rotting logs or plants.

Parrots' necks are very flexible so they can get their heads into just about anything!

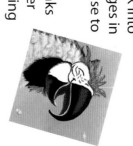

Where in the world?

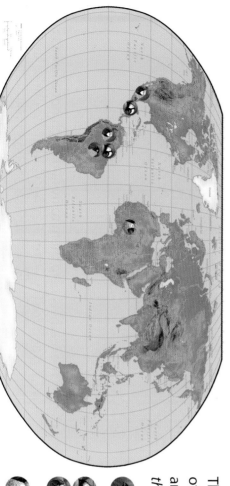

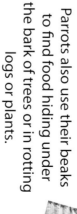

There are over 300 different types, or species, of parrots. Four of the different types of parrots are shown in this book. *See if you can find where these parrots come from on the map.*

Nanday conures (green) are from South America, south of the Amazon region.

Scarlet Macaws and Blue and Gold Macaws are both from Central and South American rainforests.

African Grey Parrots are from equatorial Africa.

Make-a-Beak Craft

Top Beak

Bottom Beak

Top Beak

Bottom Beak

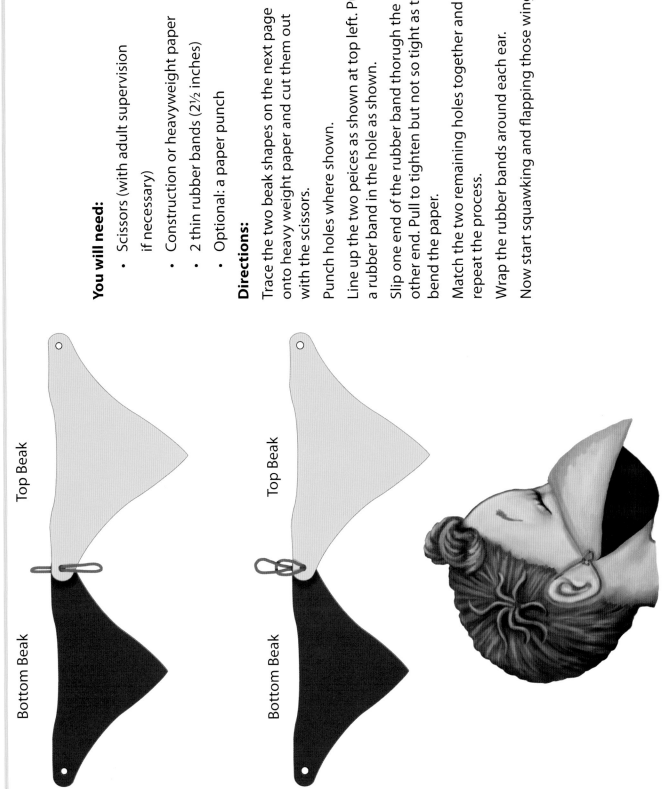

You will need:

- Scissors (with adult supervision if necessary)
- Construction or heavyweight paper
- 2 thin rubber bands (2½ inches)
- Optional: a paper punch

Directions:

Trace the two beak shapes on the next page onto heavy weight paper and cut them out with the scissors.

Punch holes where shown.

Line up the two peices as shown at top left. Put a rubber band in the hole as shown.

Slip one end of the rubber band thorugh the other end. Pull to tighten but not so tight as to bend the paper.

Match the two remaining holes together and repeat the process.

Wrap the rubber bands around each ear.

Now start squawking and flapping those wings!

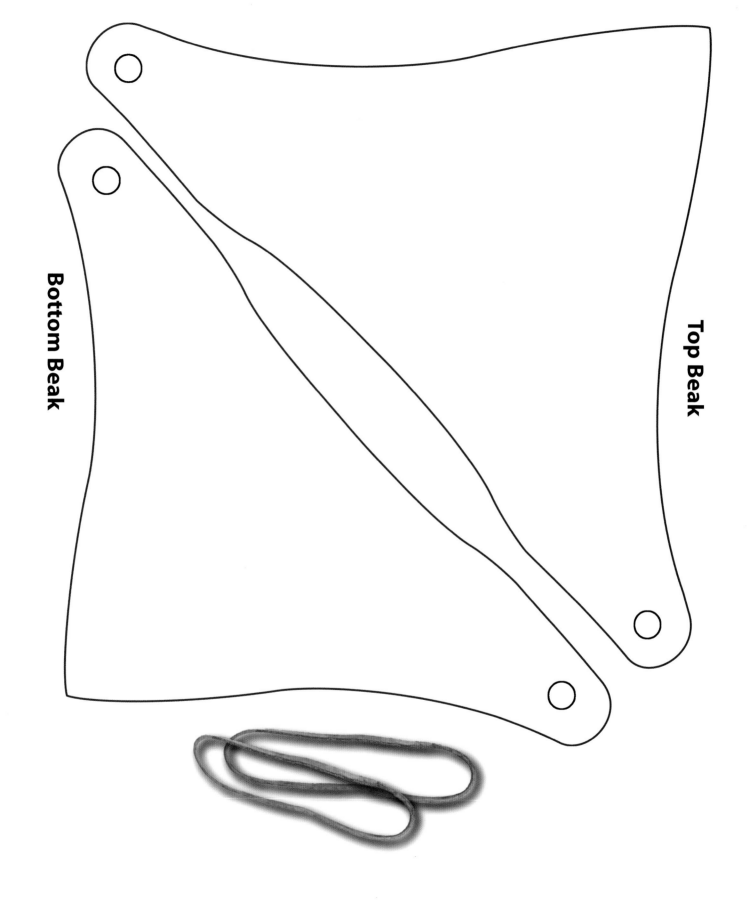

Top Beak

Bottom Beak

Are you ready for a pet parrot?

Parrots make wonderful pets, but they are not for everyone. If you would like to share your home with a pet parrot, make sure you are ready to give it everything it needs. And keep in mind that this may be a lifetime commitment, as some parrots grow to be older than humans! Most parrots are intelligent and affectionate and some like to be with people, but they can be very noisy and very demanding. Most of all they need your love and dedication to be healthy and happy. Make sure you get your parrot from a bird breeder with a good reputation. Often parrots are smuggled in from the wild and sold as pets. That hurts wild parrot populations and has made some species endangered. You could also get a pet parrot from one of the many parrot rescue and adoption agencies. There are lots of pet parrots that need good homes.

Cleanliness

Parrots love to make a mess. They throw their food around while they eat. Often the food lands outside the cage. This is natural behavior for a parrot, but it means extra cleaning work for you.

A Cage

Your parrot needs a nice cage, even though it won't want to spend all its time there. The parrot's cage is its place to rest, eat, sleep, and feel safe. The cage needs to be big enough for the parrot to open its wings, and tall enough for the parrot to climb around. It needs to be sturdy enough to resist the parrot's chewing. (parrots chew everything). And, the bars on the cage need to be close enough together so a parrot's head can't get stuck in them.

Noise

Parrots have loud voices, and they love to use them. It is natural behavior for them. They need to have owners (and neighbors) who don't mind hearing a bit of squawking everyday.

Food

Most parrots love to eat seeds, but they can't live on seeds alone. They need a variety of food, especially fresh fruit and vegetables. Wash these carefully before you feed them to your pet. Pellets are also important because they offer balanced nutrition for the bird. You can buy them at a pet store. Never feed your parrot chocolate, tomato, or avocado.

Toys

Parrots love to play and chew. You can buy parrot toys at the pet store. You can also find things around your house that your parrot will like to play with. Scraps of paper, phone books, magazines, untreated wood blocks, empty paper towel rolls, and wooden spoons are good examples. Make sure these things are clean and don't contain any plastic, toxic paint or other harmful material.

Veterinarians

There are avian veterinarians that are specially trained to care for birds. Ask your vet if he/she is so trained or look in the yellow pages or on the internet to find one. As with any type of pet, it is important to take your parrot to a vet on a regular basis for checkups.

Time

Parrots don't like being alone, so your parrot will want to spend a lot of time with you.